Be An Expert!™

Rescue Vehicles

Erin Kelly

Children's Press®
An imprint of Scholastic Inc.

Contents

Know the Names

Be an expert! Get to know the names of these rescue vehicles.

POLICE

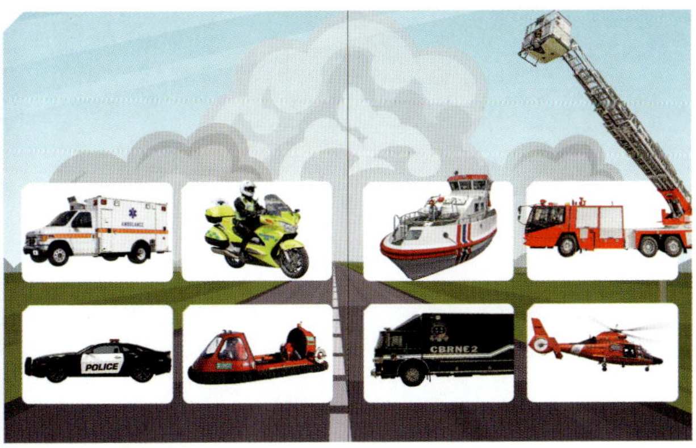

Fire Trucks

Here they come. They are ready to put out the fire!

pumper truck

Zoom In

Find these parts in the big picture.

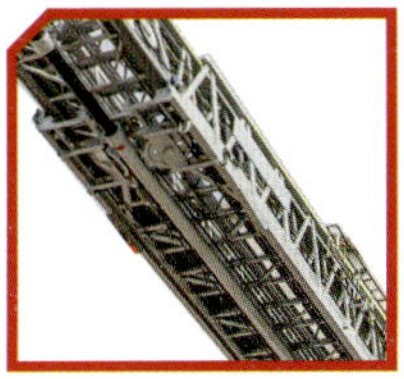

ladder

hose

bucket

flashing lights

ladder truck

fire chief SUV

Ambulances

Wee woo! Wee woo!
Cars, get out of the way!

Expert Fact

Sick or **injured** people ride in the back. They get to the hospital fast!

Police Cars

They rush to a crime!

Quick Question

Q: How do you talk to other police?

A: Each car has a **police radio**. You press a button and talk into it.

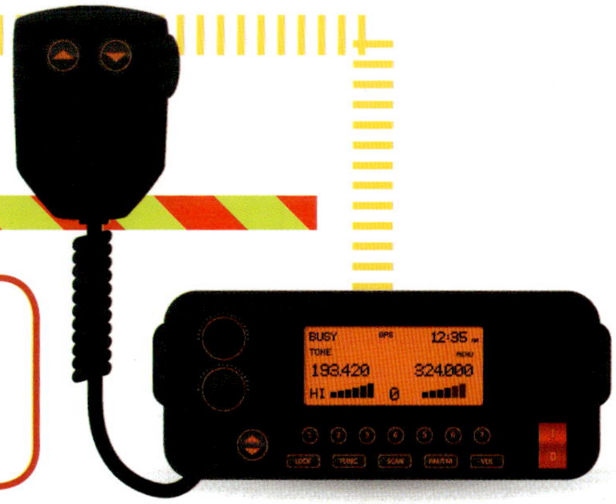

Coast Guard Boats

They help other boats in trouble.

Expert Fact

This boat is special. If it flips over in a storm, it turns back over!

Rescue Helicopters

They can lift a hurt person.

Zoom In

Find these parts in the big picture.

blades

wheels

hoist

searchlight

RAF
RESCUE

Hazmat Trucks

They clean up bad spills!

Quick Question

Q: What does *hazmat* mean?

A: It means **hazardous** materials. Stay away!

Motorcycle Ambulances

They get through **traffic** fast!

Expert Fact

The drivers get special training. They know how to help people who are hurt.

Hydrocopters

They can go over water, ice, snow, or land.

Quick Question

Q: Where are hydrocopters used?

A: They rescue people in icy waters. Most vehicles would get stuck or sink, but not the hydrocopter!

All the Vehicles

Everybody is safe.
Thanks, rescue vehicles!

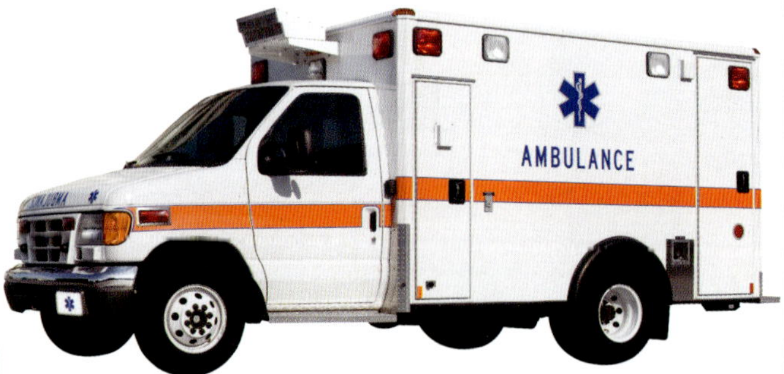

1.

2.

5.

6.

Expert Quiz

Do you know the names of these rescue vehicles? Then you are an expert! See if someone else can name them too!

3.

4.

7.

8.

Answers: 1. Ambulance. 2. Motorcycle ambulance. 3. Coast Guard boat. 4. Fire truck. 5. Police car. 6. Hydrocopter. 7. Hazmat truck. 8. Rescue helicopter.

Expert Gear

Meet an emergency medical technician, or EMT. What does she need to help people?

She has a **stethoscope**.

She has a **penlight**.

She has **gloves**.

She has a **first aid kit**.

Glossary

hazardous (HAZ-ur-duhs): dangerous or risky.

injured (IN-jurd): harmed or hurt.

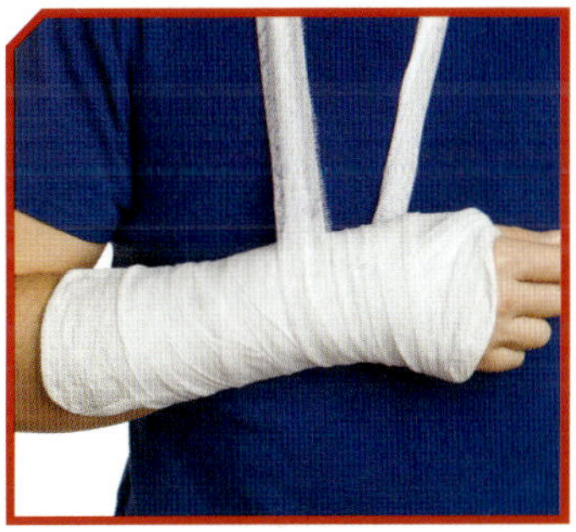

police radio (puh-LEES RAY-dee-oh): a device police use to talk to each other.

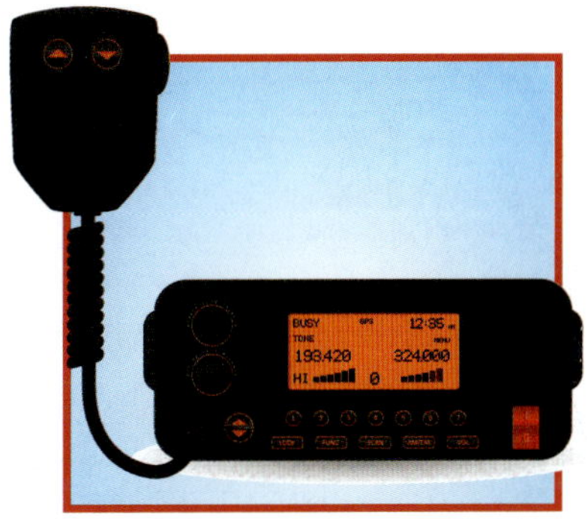

traffic (TRAF-ik): vehicles moving on a road or highway.

Index

A CIP catalog record of this book is available from the Library of Congress.
ISBN 978-0-531-13052-0 (library binding) 978-0-531-13157-2 (paperback)

Printed in Heshan, China 62

2 3 4 5 6 7 8 9 10 R 30 29 28 27 26 25 24 23 22 21

Scholastic Inc., 557 Broadway, New York, NY 10012.

Art direction and design by THREE DOGS DESIGN LLC.

Photos ©: cover ambulance: Adolfolazo/Dreamstime; cover police car: Rawpixel/Getty Images; 1 fire truck: CactuSoup/Getty Images; 2 bottom right: Smith Collection/Gado/Getty Images; 3 top left: Nerthuz/Dreamstime; 3 center left: Bigapplestock/Dreamstime; 3 center right: dov makabaw sundry/Alamy Images; 4 truck: David Traiforos/Dembinsky Photo Associates/Alamy Images; 7 ambulance: Tomas Hajek/Dreamstime; 9 sidebar bottom: fatihhoca/Getty Images; 9 bottom right: fstop123/Getty Images; 10-11 boat: US Coast Guard/Flickr; 11 child: AB Forces News Collection/Alamy Images; 12-13 helicopter: Ashley Cooper pics/Alamy Images; 14-15 truck: Bigapplestock/Dreamstime; 15 sidebar bottom: Dmitri Maruta/Dreamstime; 15 bottom: Martinlisner/Dreamstime; 16 motorcycle: dov makabaw sundry/Alamy Images; 18-19 hydrocopter: Ragnar Th Sigurdsson/Arctic-Images; 20 top right: dov makabaw sundry/Alamy Images; 20 bottom left: Nerthuz/Dreamstime; 20 bottom right: Smith Collection/Gado/Getty Images; 21 bottom left: Bigapplestock/Dreamstime; 22: kali9/Getty Images; 23 arm: akinshin/Getty Images; 23 traffic: Bim/Getty Images.

All other photos © Shutterstock.

Front Cover: Ambulance and Police car. **Back Cover:** Rescue Helicopter.